Meet Just William

WILLIAM'S WONDERFUL PLAN & OTHER STORIES

ILLUSTRATED BY TONY ROSS

RICHMAL CROMPTON
ADAPTED BY MARTIN JARVIS

MACMILLAN CHILDREN'S BOOKS

First published 1999 in two separate volumes as
Meet Just William: William's Wonderful Plan and Other Stories and
Meet Just William: William and the Prize Cat and Other Stories
by Macmillan Children's Books

This combined edition published 2017 by Macmillan Children's Books
an imprint of Pan Macmillan
20 New Wharf Road, London N1 9RR
Associated companies throughout the world
www.panmacmillan.com

ISBN 978-1-5098-4447-0

A CIP catalogue record for this book is available from the British Library.

Typeset by SX Composing DTP, Rayleigh, Essex
Printed and bound by CPI Group (UK) Ltd, Croydon CR0 4YY

Dear Reader

Ullo. I'm William Brown. Spect you've heard of me an' my dog Jumble cause we're jolly famous on account of all the adventures wot me an' my friends the Outlaws have.

Me an' the Outlaws try an' avoid our famlies cause they don' unnerstan' us. Specially my big brother Robert an' my rotten sister Ethel. She's awful. An' my parents are really <u>hartless</u>. Y'know, my father stops my pocket-money for no reason at all, an' my mother never lets me keep pet rats or <u>anythin'</u>.

It's jolly hard bein' an Outlaw an' havin' adventures when no one unnerstan's you, I can tell you.

You can read all about me, if you like, in this excitin' an' speshul new collexion of all my fav'rite stories. I hope you have a jolly gud time readin' 'em.

Yours truly

William Brown

WILLIAM'S WONDERFUL PLAN

& OTHER STORIES

Contents

William's Wonderful Plan   1

Parrots for Ethel   19

The Bishop's Handkerchief   41

William and St Valentine   61

William's Wonderful Plan

William noticed the caravan the first morning it appeared and formed his plans at once for acquaintance with its owners.

Caravans had a peculiar fascination for William. He had always found in caravan-dwellers, whether of gypsy or bohemian persuasion, a pleasing freedom from the conventions and prejudices of regular house-holders.

Immediately after school he made his way down to the caravan and hung about it. He could see a man in the next field seated at an easel, painting.

1

William was just about to draw closer to the caravan when a little girl appeared suddenly in the doorway. She was about William's age with a round, dimpled face and dark curls.

"What are you doing there, boy?" said the little girl in a clear voice. "Come and help me wash up."

Impressed despite himself by the imperiousness of the little girl's voice, William managed to preserve his manly independence so far as to reply, with a swaggering laugh, "Huh, you needn't try bossing me, 'cause I'm jolly well not goin' to be bossed by any ole girl."

But, even as he said it, he was turning to make his way meekly to the caravan, and within a few minutes was engaged in washing up and sweeping out the tiny room under the little girl's orders.

She informed him, while he did so, that she had had measles, and that this caravan holiday with her father was her final convalescence, before she returned to school.

"My father," she informed him, "is the greatest artist in the world. He can cook, too, but he's very untidy."

And she bustled about, dusting, tidying, putting away the tea things.

She was certainly not William's ideal caravan-dweller. On the other hand, her dimples were distinctly attractive, and William found her imperious manner intriguing.

After that, he called there regularly. He had become the little girl's willing slave. The artist addressed him vaguely as "boy" whenever he

3

met him, and seemed to feel no curiosity about him.

William had told no one about the caravan and its occupants, but he soon found that the news had spread through the village.

Mrs Bott, of the Hall, coming to invite William to a children's garden party, added, "And I'm going to ask that little girl who's camping here with her father. He's quite distinguished, I hear. An RA and all that . . ."

When Mrs Bott had gone, William, who hated visits to the Hall, did his best to extricate himself from the festivity.

"I'm sure I shan't be well enough," he pleaded to his mother. "It's no good me goin' there with an illness comin' on, an' givin' it to everyone there."

"But you haven't got an illness, William," protested his mother.

"I din' say I'd got one jus' this minute. I only said I felt I was goin' to have one that afternoon. I mean it doesn't seem fair to people to say you'll go to a place when you *know* you're only goin' to give them all an illness."

"If you think you're going to be ill, William, I'll ask the doctor to call."

William beat a hasty retreat.

To his surprise, the little girl actually wanted to go to the party.

"Don't be silly, William," she said. "Of *course* I want to go. It's a *party*. The only thing is . . ."

She sighed and the sparkle died away from her face.

"Yes?" said William.

"I haven't got a proper party dress . . . I've just got an old muslin one, all washed out and ever so much too short . . . and all the others will have lovely dresses. I shan't enjoy it a bit . . ."

"Well, don't go then," said William.

She stamped her small foot. "Don't be *silly*. I tell you I *want* to go."

"Well, ask your father to get you a new dress."

"No, I won't. He's poor and he's working hard and he mustn't be worried. You see, the one I have does all right for school but it'll look *awful* at a garden party, because I *know* all the others will have nicer ones."

"Now, look here," said William impulsively, "don't you worry. I'll see that you have a nice party dress for it."

He was aghast when he heard himself make this astounding offer, but it was too late to retract. Her face beamed with joy.

"Oh, William! Will you *really*?"

He found her gratitude very pleasing.

"'Course I will," he said, with a short laugh. "A little thing like that's nothin' to me. Nothin' at all."

"But William, you mustn't let anyone know you're getting it for me, will you? I should feel like a beggar if you did."

William gave another short laugh.

"Oh, no," he said. "'Course I wouldn't do that. Oh no. I'll get you a jolly nice new party dress, a jolly nice new one. You needn't worry about *that*."

The little girl beamed once more.

"Oh, William!" she said. "You are wonderful."

"Mother," he said thoughtfully that evening. "I don't mind goin' to this party of Mrs Bott's, if I can go in fancy dress."

"But of *course* you can't go in fancy dress, William," said his mother firmly. "It isn't a fancy dress party."

7

"P'raps it is, and she forgot to say. Anyway, I think I ought to have a fancy dress ready, case it is."

"But William, what *nonsense*! And even if it is, you've got your Red Indian suit."

"I'm sick of that ole Red Indian suit. I want to go as a little girl. I want you to buy me a little girl's party dress, so that if we find it's fancy dress at the last minute, I can go in it."

"William, I can't think what's come over you."

"Nothin's come over me. Surely I can go to a fancy dress party as a little girl if I want to."

"But there is no fancy dress party," protested Mrs Brown again.

"Well, will you give me a little girl's party dress and count it my Christmas present?"

"No, William, no, and I've no time to stay here talking nonsense with you like this. I've got the lunch to see to."

William decided to approach the six-year-old Violet Elizabeth Bott in whose honour the garden party was being held.

He thought of the endless succession of elaborate frocks in which her small person made its appearance at all the local functions.

She was, of course, much smaller than the little girl of the caravan, but surely, thought William, the little girl could make one dress for herself out of two of Violet Elizabeth's.

He approached the Hall cautiously and found Violet Elizabeth sitting on an upturned wheelbarrow.

"I'm a princess, William," she announced with her habitual lisp. "An' you're my subject. You've got to bow when you speak to me."

Ordinarily, William would have ignored her, but to the lady's gratification and secret surprise he bowed.

"Look here," he began, "I want to ask you something."

"You must say 'Your Royal Highness' when you speak to me," said Violet Elizabeth imperiously.

"Your Royal Highness," muttered William. "Look here . . . I want to ask you—"

Violet Elizabeth had leapt from the wheelbarrow.

"I want to go for a ride," she said. "Make my throne into a chariot."

William obediently turned over the wheelbarrow.

"Now, look here," he said. "What I want to ask you—"

"Now you're my coachman," said Violet Elizabeth, reposing on the wheelbarrow and arranging her miniature skirt about her with dignity. "Give me a ride, coachman."

Still forcing his proud spirit to this uncongenial servitude, William took up the handles of the wheelbarrow, and began to push the small tyrant round the lawn.

"Now, look here," he began again rather breathlessly. "This is what I wanted to ask you—"

"You must say 'Your Royal Highness' when you speak to me," said Violet Elizabeth. "If you don't, I'll have your head chopped off for treason. And go faster!"

"Your Royal Highness," said William. "Now this is what I wanted to ask you—"

"I'm having a new frock from London for our party," announced Violet Elizabeth.

It was a heaven-sent opening.

"I say," panted William, "you've got lots of party frocks, haven't you?"

"Hundreds an' hundreds, an' say 'Your Royal Highness' or I'll have you arrested for treason."

"Your Royal Highness – well now, suppose there was another little girl—"

Violet Elizabeth's interest was suddenly aroused.

"Yes. Go on."

"Suppose there was another little girl that was invited to your party, but had only got a very old frock to come in, wouldn't you want to give her some of your old party frocks so that she can have a nice one to come in?"

A seraphic smile appeared upon Violet Elizabeth's angel countenance.

"No, I wouldn't," she said. "I'd *like* her to come in an old frock, 'cause it would make my new frock seem smarter than ever."

There was only one thing to do and William did it. He tipped the young autocrat urgently out of the wheelbarrow on the lawn, then set off himself quickly down the drive.

For a second, fury and amazement deprived Violet Elizabeth of the power of speech. Then it returned and scream after shrill scream rent the peaceful summer morning.

William was slowly approaching the caravan. He had almost decided to admit failure, but when the little girl came running across the field to him he could not find it in his heart to disappoint her.

"Oh, William," she cried excitedly. "Have you got it?"

"Er – not yet," said William, trying rather unsuccessfully to assume an airy manner. "There's plenty of time."

"You have got a plan, haven't you, William?" she said, anxiously.

He laughed a carefree laugh that rang slightly hollow.

"'Course I have," he said. "I should jolly well think I've got a plan all right."

They reached the caravan, and he followed her into it. A much-washed white muslin dress lay over a chair. The little girl held it up.

"It looks *awful*," she said sorrowfully. "I'd rather go in it than not go at all, of course, but

I shall feel dreadful if I have to wear it. It's all washed to bits and it's miles too small. But – you *have* promised to get me a new one, haven't you, William?"

"Oh yes," said William with a ghastly smile. "Oh yes, don't you worry about that."

The church clock struck five. She flung the dress over the chair again.

"That's tea-time. I'd better go and fetch Father. Be an angel, William, and put on the kettle. The water's in the petrol tin, you know."

She ran off across the field and William, heavy-hearted, lit the spirit-lamp as he had seen the little girl do, and filled the kettle from the petrol tin.

He had often seen the little girl fill the kettle from the petrol tin, but he had never realised that the caravan contained two petrol tins, one full of water, the other of paraffin, and it was from the paraffin tin that William had filled the kettle.

The next few moments were like the climax

of a nightmare. As he placed the kettle on the spirit stand a sheet of flame burst out, precipitating him through the caravan door and on to the grass outside.

Through a whirligig of stars, he saw two men who happened to be passing leap into the caravan and fling their coats upon the bright sheet of flame.

The flame died down. Through eddies of smoke William, sitting with a blackened face and singed hair upon the grass, saw the scorched remnants of the little girl's dress,

now about the size of a pocket handkerchief, still reposing on the chair.

He gazed at it for a few moments, sprang to his feet, and fled from the scene of ruin.

For the next few days he felt as if he were still living in a nightmare. He dare not revisit the little girl; his brain seemed to be numbed and stupefied by the immensity of the catastrophe.

The day of the garden party arrived. He could think of nothing but the little girl, deprived by his act of the party to which she had been looking forward.

She had said that she would rather go in the old muslin dress than not go at all. And he had burnt the old muslin dress.

He walked slowly and in a hangdog fashion towards the Hall. The little girl would not be at the party, of course, but suppose she were waiting outside to reproach him . . .

He entered the gate, and crossed over the lawn to a group of little boys and gaily dressed little girls.

Suddenly he heard a cry of "William", and to his amazement he saw the little girl detach herself from the group and come across the lawn to him. She wore a very pretty and obviously new dress of pale pink.

"Oh, *William*," she was saying, "you are *wonderful*! Oh, William, thank you so much. It was so clever of you, and I'm so sorry that I didn't really believe you'd got a plan. And it was such a *wonderful* plan."

William was gazing at her, open-mouthed.

"W-w-w-w-what?" he demanded.

"Why, to burn my old dress so that the insurance people should give me a new one. They've given me a lovely new one, haven't they? Oh, William, it was so clever of you to think of it."

William recovered himself quickly. He assumed his easy swagger, smiling at her in affectionate condescension.

"Oh, that's all right," he said. "A little thing like that's nothin' to me."

Parrots for Ethel

"Now," said William to Douglas and Ginger, "'bout this animal lecture what I'm going to give. We'll have it in our summer-house, an' I'll lecture on 'em. An' we'll have all our cats and Jumble. And we'll colleck some more insecks, an' we'll have Ginger's dormouse."

"Right," said Ginger, "let's go and fetch the dormouse."

They passed the drawing-room where Ethel sat with George and Hector. George was Douglas's elder brother; Hector was Ginger's. Both young men were infatuated with Ethel.

"Douglas drove me half-mad with a beastly

mouth organ yesterday," groaned George, "till I took it from him and chucked it into the pond."

"Same here with Ginger's trumpet," said Hector.

"Well I'm sure no boy ever was half as bad as William," said Ethel with a sigh. "He broke a vase that was one of my greatest treasures yesterday with his bow and arrow. I confiscated them of course."

Both Hector and George made an inarticulate murmur of deep sympathy.

"And William had a thing," said Ethel dreamily, "that was supposed to sound like a bird chirping. Only it didn't. It went through and *through* my head."

"Oh what a *shame*," said Hector and George simultaneously, in passionate indignation.

"I'm very fond of birds," continued Ethel.

"What sort do you like best?"

"I think that parrots are rather sweet," said Ethel. "Don't you?"

Neither spoke.

"I remember once," went on Ethel, "a friend of mine had to go into quarantine for measles, or something like that, and a friend of hers gave her a parrot to be comforting for her. He gave it in rather a nice way, too. He put it on the garden seat on the lawn, and sent in a letter to say that if she'd look out of her window she would see a little friend who had come to keep her company. Or something like that. She was always devoted to that parrot."

*

It was the next morning. Ethel was staring wildly at a letter she held in her hand.

"Daphne's got measles, and I was with her last night. Oh, what shall I do?"

"You'll have to go into quarantine, I'm afraid, dear," said her mother placidly.

William received the news without emotion. A more terrible tragedy had happened than Ethel's quarantine. Ginger's dormouse had died in the night.

Ginger and Douglas took the dead body to the summer-house, leaving William alone on the lawn, gloomily considering the prospect of his lecture thus deprived of its star turn.

He didn't at first see Ginger's brother Hector who had come round to the side of the house looking pale and distraught.

"This is terrible news," began Hector.

"Yes, isn't it?" said William. "Terrible."

"She seemed all right yesterday," continued Hector.

"She was, she was quite all right yesterday.

I think it was eatin' those berries."

"What berries?"

"Those berries Ginger gave her."

"Wha—? Did Ginger give her some berries?"

"Oh yes, all sorts of different coloured kinds of berries what he found about the garden and she ate them all."

"But I heard in the village it was measles."

"No, it's worse than measles. She's dead. She died in the night."

"*What?*"

"She's dead. When Ginger 'n' me came to clean out her cage this morning we found her dead."

"Clean out her c—? What the dickens are you talking about?"

"Our mouse," said William. "Weren't you?"

The visitor controlled himself with an effort.

"No. I was talking about your sister, Ethel."

"Oh, Ethel. Oh no. No, it's not measles, it's somethin' else. Quarantine or somethin'."

Hector turned on his heel and strode away. He'd remembered suddenly what Ethel had said. He'd get her a parrot.

William remained upon the garden bench, plunged in gloom. The voice of George broke upon his meditations.

"Well, I'm very sorry to hear this," began George.

William's heart warmed to him. Here, at any rate, was sympathy.

"Yes," he said. "Yes, it was an awful shock to us all to find her dead this mornin'."

"*What?*"

Explanation followed, and George walked quickly down the road. He'd suddenly remembered what Ethel had said about the parrot yesterday. He'd get her one.

William rejoined the others in the summer-house.

"Tell you what. We'll put up a notice asking people to lend us an'mals, or give us an'mals, like what they do to the zoo."

Ten minutes later they gathered round to look at William's notice. It read as follows:

"mister william brown is going to leckcher on anmals and will be gratful to anyone who will give or lend him anmals to be leckchered on mister william brown is out now lookin for valubul insex, but will be back before dinner mister william brown will be glad if people givin him anmals to be leckchered on will put them on the seat in the back garden an tie them up if they are savvidge anmals mister william brown's vallubul assistunts are ginger and douglas."

They pinned the notice on the side gate and sallied forth in search of insects.

A short time before their return, Hector appeared looking very hot and breathless. He held a parrot in a cage.

He had cycled frenziedly into the nearest town and had spent practically his last penny on it. He found a garden seat conveniently situated.

He then slipped a letter quietly through the letter box. In the letter he said that if she would look out of the window, she would see upon the garden seat a little friend who had come to keep her company.

Then, smiling fatuously to himself, he tip-toed away.

Hardly had he disappeared, when the Outlaws returned. They had found only one species of caterpillar.

They turned the corner of the house, and there upon the garden seat was a parrot in a cage. They rushed to it and bore it off in triumph to the summer-house.

The parrot uttered a shrill scream of laughter, and said with deep feeling, "Go away, I hate you."

"Wonder what they eat?" said Ginger.

"I say, where's that tin with my caterpillar in?" said William. "Who's took it?"

"You left it on the garden seat, when we fetched the parrot in," said Douglas.

They hurried out to the garden seat.

It was empty.

Meanwhile, a housemaid had found Hector's note on the mat and taken it up to Ethel's room. Ethel's room did not happen to overlook the garden. She read the note with a smile, almost as fatuous as Hector's.

"A little friend to keep you company." Oh, it was very, very sweet of him. She opened the door, and called to the housemaid.

"Emma, will you bring me something that you'll find upon the garden seat."

Emma went out and returned with a small

tin. Inside were several leaves and a big furry caterpillar.

"Oh, *that's* his idea of being funny, is it?" said Ethel viciously. "Well, it's not *mine*."

And she flung the tin furiously into the fire-place.

At that very moment, the faithful George was tiptoeing softly round the side of the house, bearing a parrot in a cage, and the Outlaws were returning from another cater-pillar expedition.

"Funny we only caught one of those caterpillars again," said William.

"Well, one's enough to lecture on, I suppose," said Douglas.

William had stopped suddenly, and was staring in blank amazement.

"There – there's another parrot on the seat. Look. It is, isn't it? It *is* another parrot, isn't it?"

"Yes," said Ginger, "it cert'nly is. Seems sort of funny they should *all* be givin' us parrots, don't it?"

They took it into the summer-house, and the other parrot greeted it with a sardonic laugh. The latecomer gazed round with a supercilious air, and finally screamed, "Great Scott."

Then William said, "Where's that tin with the caterpillar in?"

"You left it on the bench again, William," said Douglas.

They went out and stood around the empty bench.

"*Well*," said William, "it's mos' *mysterious*. Someone's pinched this one too."

Upstairs Ethel was hurling the second caterpillar and tin furiously into the fireplace.

It was late afternoon. Hector, still wearing his fatuous smile, came round the corner of the house. He felt that he couldn't wait a minute longer without hearing an account of Ethel's rapturous glee on the receipt of his present.

A housemaid opened the door.

"I just called to see if the parrot was settling down all right," said Hector.

"The parrot?"

"Yes. The parrot that arrived this morning."

"No parrot arrived this morning, sir."

"W-what? Are you sure?"

"Oh quite sure, sir. There's no parrot in the house at all."

"Not – er – not in Miss Brown's room?"

"Oh no, sir. I've just been there."

Dazedly, Hector walked away. Then he

stopped. There, just outside the closed door of the summer-house, stood William with a parrot in a cage.

The two parrots had begun to hold a screaming contest, till William was forced to take George's outside.

Hector's first impulse was to hurl himself upon William and accuse him of stealing his parrot, but on approaching nearer he saw that it was not his parrot, and it was not his cage.

"Whose is that parrot, William?" he asked pleasantly.

"Mine," said William.

"W-where did you get it?" said Hector still more pleasantly.

"Someone gave it to me."

There was a short silence.

Then Hector said, "I'm – I'm willing to buy that parrot from you, William."

A sudden gleam had come into William's eye.

"I tell you what I'll do. I'll swap it with you."

"What for?" said Hector hopefully.

"I want to give Ginger a present. One of those nice trumpets. You can get them at Foley's in the village. They cost six shillings. I'll swap it with you for one of those trumpets to give to Ginger."

For a minute there was murder in Hector's eye, then he gulped and said, "Very well. You wait here."

Soon he was back with the trumpet. He hurled it at William, seized the parrot cage and disappeared. He was going to write a beautiful little note, fasten it to the cage, and deliver it in person at the front door.

Inside the summer-house the Outlaws were dancing a dance of exultation around Ginger, who was producing loud but discordant strains from his magnificent new trumpet.

This festive gathering was, however, broken by the sudden advent of George. Like Hector, he'd been informed that no parrot had entered the house that day.

He then caught a glimpse of the Outlaws in

the summer-house, leaping wildly about a parrot in a cage.

"You little *thieves*," he panted. "What do you *mean* by taking my parrot?"

"'S not your parrot, 's ours."

George looked at the parrot. William was right. It wasn't his cage. He gulped. He began to make tentative enquiries as to the exact value William set upon his parrot.

It appeared that William was willing to exchange it for a mouth organ, one of the six shilling ones from Foley's, because he wanted to give one to Douglas as a present.

George went off furiously to buy the mouth organ, returned with it, flung it at the Outlaws and stalked off with his parrot.

At a discreet distance, the Outlaws followed George round and out of the side gate. George was going to take the parrot in at the front door, ring the bell, and deliver it in person.

And then, to his amazement, he saw Hector blithely approaching from the opposite direction, also carrying a parrot in a cage.

They met at the gate. Each recognised his own parrot and cage in the hand of the other.

Simultaneously they shouted, "So *you* stole my parrot!"

The Outlaws watched in mystified delight. A shabby-looking man who happened to be passing also stopped to form an interested audience.

George turned round, thrust the cage into William's arms with a curt, "Take that", and began to roll up his sleeves.

Hector turned to the shabby-looking man, thrust his cage into his arms, and the next minute, George and Hector were giving a splendid boxing display upon the high road with bare fists.

The shabby man crept softly away with his parrot and cage. Very thoughtfully, William carried his cage up to Ethel's room.

"Erm, I won't come in, Ethel," he said, "'cause of catching your quarantine illness, but I've brought you a little present. I heard you said you'd like a parrot, and I brought you one."

Ethel was deeply touched. "How very kind of you, William," she said. "I – er – you can have your bow and arrow back. I'm sorry I took it from you. It's very kind of you to bring me the parrot."

Willliam received his bow and arrow with perfunctory thanks. Just at that moment the housemaid came up with a note. Ethel tore it open.

"Why, it's all right," she said. "Daphne hasn't got measles after all. The rash has all gone. And the doctor said she's not got it at all. And they want me to go to tea. And they've got that handsome artist coming. Oh, how jolly. I'll start at once."

A few minutes later, Ethel, accompanied by William, Ginger and Douglas, set out from the front door. At the gate Hector and George came forward to greet them.

The fight was just over, abandoned by mutual consent. Ethel passed them head in air. They stood, gaping after her in helpless bewilderment.

The Outlaws turned back to look at them. Ginger and Douglas raised trumpet and mouth organ to their lips and uttered defiant strains. William waved his bow and arrow in careless greeting.

They had had a most successful day. There had been, it's true, certain mysterious elements in it that they couldn't understand, but that didn't matter. They were perfectly happy.

The Bishop's Handkerchief

Until now William had taken no interest in his handkerchiefs as accessories. But last week, Ginger (a member of the circle known to themselves as the Outlaws, of which William was the leader) had received a handkerchief as a birthday present from an aunt in London.

William, on hearing the news, had jeered, but the sight of the handkerchief had silenced him. It was a large handkerchief, larger than William had conceived it possible for handkerchiefs to be. It was made of silk, and contained all the colours of the rainbow.

41

Round the edge, green dragons sported upon a red ground.

Ginger displayed it, fully prepared for scorn and merriment, but there was something about the handkerchief that impressed them all . . .

The next morning Henry appeared with a handkerchief almost exactly like it, and the day after that Douglas had one. William felt his prestige lowered. He – the born leader – was the only one of the select circle who did not possess a coloured silk handkerchief.

That evening he approached his mother.

"I don't think white ones is much use," he said.

"Don't scrape your feet on the carpet, William," said his mother placidly. "I thought white ones were the only tame kind – not that I think your father will let you have any more. You know what he said when they got all over the floor and bit his finger."

"I'm not talkin' about *rats*," said William. "I'm talkin' about handkerchiefs."

"Oh – handkerchiefs! White ones are far the best. There's nothing better than white linen."

"Pers'nally," said William with a judicial air, "I think silk's better than linen, an' white's so tirin' to look at. I think a kind of colour's better for your eyes. My eyes do ache a bit sometimes. I think it's prob'ly with keep lookin' at white handkerchiefs."

"Don't be silly, William. I'm not going to

buy you silk handkerchiefs to get covered with mud and ink and coal, as yours do . . ."

William decided to investigate Robert's bedroom. He opened Robert's dressing-table drawer and turned over the handkerchiefs.

He caught his breath with surprise and pleasure. There, beneath all Robert's other handkerchiefs, was a larger, silkier, more multi-coloured handkerchief than Ginger's or Douglas's or Henry's.

He gazed at it in ecstatic joy. He slipped it into his pocket and, standing before the looking glass, took it out with a flourish, shaking its lustrous folds.

He was absorbed in this occupation when Robert entered.

"What do you think *you're* doing?"

"Oh, I jus' wanted to borrow a handkerchief, Robert. I thought you wun't mind lendin' me this handkerchief."

"Well, I would," said Robert curtly. "Give it back to me."

Reluctantly William handed it back to Robert.

"How much'll you give it me for?" he said.

"Well, how much have you?" said Robert, ruthlessly.

"Nothin' – jus' at present," admitted William. "But I'd *do* something for you for it. I'd do anythin' you want done for it. You just tell me what to do for it, an' I'll *do* it."

"Well, you can – you can get the Bishop's handkerchief for me, and then I'll give mine to you."

The trouble with Robert was that he imagined himself a wit.

The trouble with William was that he took things literally.

The Bishop was expected in the village the next day. It was the great event of the summer. He was a distant relation of the Vicar's.

He was to open the Fête, address a large meeting on Temperance, spend the night at the vicarage, and depart the next morning.

The Bishop was a fatherly, simple-minded old man of seventy. He enjoyed the Fête, except for one thing. Wherever he looked, he met the gaze of a freckled untidy frowning small boy.

He could not understand it. The boy seemed to be everywhere. The boy seemed to follow him about . . .

Then he addressed the meeting on Temperance, his audience consisting chiefly of adults. But in the front seat, the same earnest frowning boy fixed him with a determined gaze . . .

After the meeting William wandered down the road to the Vicarage. He pondered gloomily over his wasted afternoon. Fate had not thrown the Bishop's handkerchief in his path. But he did not yet despair.

He looked cautiously through the Vicarage hedge. Nothing was to be seen. He crawled inside the garden and round to the back of the house. The Bishop was tired after his address. He lay outstretched upon a deckchair beneath a tree.

Over the head and face of His Lordship, was stretched a large super-fine linen handkerchief. William's set expression brightened. On hands and knees he began to crawl through the grass, towards the portly form.

Crouching behind the chair, he braced himself for the crime; he measured the distance between the chair and the garden gate.

One, two, three – then suddenly the portly form stirred, the handkerchief was firmly withdrawn by a podgy hand, and a dignified voice yawned and said, "Heigh-ho!"

At the same moment the Bishop sat up. William, from his refuge behind the chair, looked wildly round. The door of the house was opening. There was only one thing to do.

William was as nimble as a monkey. Like a flash of lightning he disappeared up a tree. It was a very leafy tree. It completely concealed William, but William had a good bird's eye view of the world beneath him.

The Vicar came out rubbing his hands.

"You rested, my Lord?" he said.

"I'm afraid I've had forty winks," said His Lordship pleasantly. "Just dropped off, you know. I dreamt about that boy who was at the meeting this afternoon."

"What boy, my Lord?" asked the Vicar.

"I noticed him at the Fête and the meeting. He looked – he looked a soulful boy. I dare say you know him."

The Vicar considered.

"I can't think of any boy round here like that," he said.

The Bishop sighed.

"It seemed an earnest *questing* face – as if the boy wanted something – *needed* something. I hope my little talk helped him."

"Without doubt it did, my Lord," said the Vicar, politely. "I thought we might dine out here – the days draw out so pleasantly now."

The Vicar went to order dinner in the garden. The Bishop drew the delicate handkerchief once more over his rubicund features.

The breast of the Bishop on the lawn began to rise and sink. The figure of the Vicar was visible at the study window, as he gazed with fond pride upon the slumbers of his distinguished guest.

William dared not descend in view of that watching figure. Finally, it sat down in a chair by the window, and began to read a book.

William took from his pocket a bent pin attached to a piece of string. This apparatus lived permanently in his pocket, because he had not given up hope of catching a trout in the village stream.

He lowered this cautiously and drew the bent pin carefully on the white linen expanse.

Leaning down from his leafy retreat, William drew the bent pin sharply across. It missed the handkerchief and caught the Bishop's ear.

The Bishop sat up with a scream. William, pin and string withdrew into the shade of the branches.

The Vicar ran out from the house, full of concern.

"I've been badly stung in the ear by some insect," said the Bishop. "Some virulent tropical insect, I should think – very painful. Very painful indeed—"

"My Lord," said the Vicar. "I am so sorry – so very sorry – a thousand pardons – can I procure some remedy for you – vaseline, ammonia – er – cold cream—?"

"No, no, no, no," snapped the Bishop. "I put my handkerchief over my face for a protection. If I had failed to do that I should have been even more badly stung."

The Vicar sat himself down on his chair.

The maid came out to lay the table. They watched her in silence. William shifted his position in the tree.

"Do you know," said the Bishop, "I believe that there is a cat in the tree. Several times I have heard a slight rustling."

It would have been better for William to

remain silent, but William's genius occasionally misled him. He was anxious to prevent the investigation; to prove once and for all his identity as a cat.

He leant forward and uttered a re-echoing "Mi-*aw-aw-aw!*"

As imitations go, it was rather good.

There was a slight silence. Then, "It *is* a cat," said the Bishop in triumph.

"Excuse me, my Lord," said the Vicar.

He went softly into the house and returned holding a shoe.

"This will settle his feline majesty," he smiled.

Then he hurled the shoe violently into the tree.

"Sh! Scoot!" he said as he did it.

William was annoyed. The shoe narrowly missed his face. He secured it and waited.

"I hope you haven't lost the shoe," said the Bishop anxiously.

"Oh, no. The gardener's boy will get it for me."

He settled himself in his chair comfortably with a smile.

William leant down, held the shoe deliberately over the Vicar's bald head then dropped it.

"*Damn!*" said the Vicar. "Excuse me, my Lord."

"H'm," said the Bishop. "Er – yes – most annoying. It lodged in a branch for a time probably, and then obeyed the force of gravity."

The Vicar was rubbing his head. William wanted to enjoy the sight of the Vicar rubbing his head. He moved a little further along the branch.

He forgot all caution. There was the sound of a rending and a crashing, and on to the table between the amazed Vicar and Bishop descended William's branch and William.

The Bishop gazed at him. "Why, that's the boy," he said.

William sat up among the debris of broken glass and crockery. He discovered that he was

bruised and that his hand was cut by one of the broken glasses.

He extricated himself from the branch and the table, and stood rubbing his bruises and sucking his hand.

"Crumbs!" was all he said.

The Vicar was gazing at him speechlessly.

"You know, my boy," said the Bishop in mild reproach, "that's a very curious thing to do – to hide up there for the purpose of eavesdropping.

"I know that you are an earnest, well-meaning little boy, and that you were interested in my address this afternoon, and I dare say you were hoping to listen to me again, but this is my time for relaxation, you know.

"Suppose the Vicar and I had been talking about something we didn't want you to hear? I'm sure you wouldn't like to listen to things people didn't want you to hear, would you?"

William stared at him in unconcealed amazement.

The Vicar, with growing memories of shoes

and "damns" and with murder in his heart, was picking up twigs and broken glass.

He knew that he could not, in the Bishop's presence, say the things to William and do the things to William that he wanted to do and say.

He contented himself with saying, "You'd better go home now. Tell your father I'll be coming to see him tomorrow."

"A well-meaning little boy, I'm sure," said the Bishop kindly. "Well-meaning, but unwise – er – unwise. But your attentiveness during the meeting did you credit, my boy – did you credit."

William turned to go. He knew when he was beaten. He had spent a lot of time and trouble and had not secured the episcopal handkerchief. He had bruised himself and cut himself.

He understood the Vicar's veiled threat. He saw all his future pocket-money vanish into nothingness with the cost of the Vicar's glasses and plates.

He wouldn't have minded if he'd got the handkerchief. He wouldn't have minded anything if—

"Don't suck your hand, my boy," said the Bishop. "An open cut like that is most dangerous. Poison works into the system by it. You remember I told you how the poison of alcohol works into the system – well, any kind of poison can work into it by a cut – don't suck it; keep it covered up – haven't you a handkerchief? Here, take mine. You needn't trouble to return it. It's an old one."

The Bishop was deeply touched by what he called the "bright spirituality" of the smile with which William thanked him.

William, limping slightly, his hand covered by a grimy rag, came out into the garden, drawing from his pocket with a triumphant flourish an enormous, violently-coloured silk handkerchief.

Robert, who was weeding the rose-bed, looked up.

"Here," he called, "you can jolly well go and put that handkerchief of mine back."

William continued his proud advance.

"'S all right," he called airily, "the Bishop's is on your dressing-table."

Robert dropped his trowel.

"Gosh!" he gasped, and hastened indoors to investigate.

William went down to the gate, smiling very slightly.

"The days are drawing out so pleasantly," he was saying to himself in a mincing accent.

"Vaseline – ammonia – er – or cold cream. Damn!"

He leant over the gate and looked up and down the road. In the distance he caught sight of the figure of his friend.

"Gin-*ger*," he yelled in hideous shrillness.

He waved his coloured handkerchief carelessly in greeting as he called. Then he swaggered out into the road . . .

William and St Valentine

Miss Lomas held a Bible class for the Sons and Daughters of Gentlefolk every Tuesday afternoon after school. Something seemed to have happened to the class since William Brown joined it. The beautiful atmosphere was destroyed.

William took his seat in the dining-room where Miss Lomas always held her class. He took a large nut out of his pocket and cracked it with his teeth.

"*Not* in here, William," said Miss Lomas faintly.

"I was goin' to put the bits of shell into my

pocket," said William. "I wasn't goin' to put 'em on your carpet or anything; but 'f you don't want me to 's all right," he said obligingly, putting nut and dismembered shell into his pocket.

"Now," said Miss Lomas brightly, "I want to give you a little talk on Brotherly Love."

"Who's St Valentine?" said William who was burrowing in his prayer book.

"Why, William?" said Miss Lomas, patiently.

"Well, his day seems to be comin', this month," said William.

Miss Lomas, with a good deal of confusion, launched into a not very clear account of the institution of St Valentine's Day.

"Well, I don't think much of *him* 's a saint," was William's verdict, "writin' soppy letters to girls instead of gettin' martyred prop'ly like Peter an' the others."

Miss Lomas put her hand to her head.

"You misunderstand me, William," she said. "What I meant to say was . . . Well, suppose we leave St Valentine till later, and have our little talk on Brotherly Love first . . . *Ow-w-w!*"

The box containing William's pet stag-beetle, Albert, had accidentally opened in William's pocket, and Albert was now taking a voyage of discovery up Miss Lomas's jumper. Miss Lomas's spectacles fell off. She tore Albert off her and rushed from the room.

William gathered up his stag-beetle and carefully examined him.

"She might have hurt him, throwing him about like that," he said sternly. "She oughter be more careful."

Then he replaced Albert tenderly in his box.

At that moment, Miss Dobson entered the room. Miss Dobson was Miss Lomas's cousin and was staying with her. Miss Dobson was very young and very pretty. She had short golden curls and blue eyes and small white teeth and an attractive smile.

"My cousin's not well enough to finish the lesson," she said. "So, I'm going to read to you all till it's time to go home. Now, let's be comfortable. Come and sit on the hearthrug. That's right. I'm going to read to you 'Scalped by the Reds'."

At the end of the first chapter, William had decided that he wouldn't mind coming to this sort of Bible class every day.

At the end of the second he had decided to marry Miss Dobson as soon as he grew up . . .

*

When William woke up the next morning, his determination to marry Miss Dobson was unchanged.

He had previously agreed quite informally to marry Joan Parfitt, his friend and play-mate and adorer, but Joan was small and dark-haired and rather silent. She was not gloriously grown-up, and tall and fair and vivacious.

William was aware that marriage must be preceded by courtship, and that courtship was an arduous business.

It was a half-holiday that afternoon and, to the consternation of his family, William announced his intention of staying at home.

He knew that Laurence Hinlock, Ethel's latest admirer, was expected for tea and William wished to study at near quarters the delicate art of courtship.

He realised that he could not marry Miss Dobson for many years to come, but he did not see why his courtship of her should not begin at once . . . He was going to learn how it was done from Laurence Hinlock and Ethel . . .

He spent the earlier part of the afternoon collecting a few more insects for his empty boxes. (He was still mourning bitterly the loss of Albert, who had been confiscated that morning by the French master.)

Then he went indoors.

There were several people in the drawing-room. He greeted them rather coldly, his eye roving round the while for what he sought.

Ethel and a tall, lank young man were sitting in the window-alcove, in two comfortable chairs, talking vivaciously and confidentially.

William took a chair and carried it over to them, put it down by the young man's chair, and sat down.

There was a short, pregnant silence.

"Good afternoon," said William, at last.

"Er – good afternoon," said the young man.

There was another silence.

"Hadn't you better go and speak to the others?" said Ethel.

"I've spoke to them," said William.

Silence again.

"I think Mrs Franks would like you to go and talk to her," said Ethel.

"No, I don't think she would," said William with perfect truth.

The young man took out a shilling and handed it to William.

"Go and buy some sweets for yourself," he said.

William put the shilling in his pocket.

"Thanks," he said. "I'll go and get them when you've all gone."

There was another and yet deeper silence. Then Ethel and the young man began to talk together again.

They had evidently decided to ignore William's presence.

William listened with rapt attention. He wanted to know what you said and the sort of voice you said it in.

"St Valentine's Day next week," said Laurence soulfully.

"Oh, no one takes any notice of that nowadays," said Ethel.

"I'm going to," said Laurence. "I think it's a beautiful idea. Its meaning, you know . . . true love . . . If I send you a Valentine, will you accept it?"

"That depends on the Valentine," said Ethel with a smile.

"It's the thought that's behind it that's the vital thing," said Laurence. "It's that that mat-

68

ters. Ethel . . . you're in all my waking dreams."

"I'm sure I'm not," said Ethel.

"You are . . . Has anyone told you before that you're a perfect Botticelli?"

"Heaps of people," said Ethel calmly.

"I was thinking about love last night," said Laurence. "Love at first sight. That's the only sort of love . . . When I first saw you, my heart leapt at the sight of you."

Laurence was a great reader of romance.

"I think that we're predestined for each other. We must have known each other in former existences. We—"

"Do speak up," said William irritably. "You're speaking so low that I can't hear what you're saying . . ."

"What do people mean by sayin' they'll send a Valentine, Mother?" said William that evening. "I thought he was a sort of saint. I don' see how you can send a saint to anyone, 'specially when he's dead 'n' in the prayer book."

"Well, it's a kind of Christmas card," said Mrs Brown vaguely, "only it's a Valentine, I mean . . . well it had gone out in my day, but I remember your grandmother showing me some that had been sent to her . . . dried ferns and flowers pasted on cardboard . . . very pretty."

"Huh!" said William. "I don' see any sense in sendin' pasted ferns, an' dead saints and things . . . But still, I'm going to do all the sort of things they do."

"What *are* you talking about, William?" said Mrs Brown.

Interest in St Valentine's Day seemed to have infected the whole household. On February 13th, William came upon his brother Robert wrapping up a large box of chocolates.

"What's that?" said William.

"A Valentine," said Robert shortly.

"Well, Miss Lomas said it was a dead saint, and Mother said it was a pasted fern, an' now you start sayin' it's a box of chocolates! No

70

one seems to know what it is. Who's it for, anyway?"

"Doreen Dobson," said Robert, answering without thinking with a glorifying blush.

"Oh, I *say*!" said William indignantly. "You can't. I've bagged her. I'm going to do a fern for her. I've had her ever since Bible class."

"Shut up and get out," said Robert.

Robert was twice William's size. William shut up and got out.

*

The Lomas family was giving a party on Saint Valentine's Day and William had been invited with Robert and Ethel. William spent two hours on his Valentine.

He could not find a fern so he picked a large spray of yew-tree instead. He found a large piece of thick cardboard, about the size of a drawing-board, and a bottle of glue in the cupboard of his father's writing-desk.

It took the whole bottle of glue, plus some flour and water, to fix the spray of yew-tree to the cardboard, and the glue mingled freely with the flour and water on William's clothing and person.

Finally, he surveyed his handiwork.

"Well, I don't see much *in* it now it's done," he said. "But I'm jolly well going to do all the things they do."

He set off to Miss Lomas's carrying his Valentine under his arm. He started out before Ethel and Robert because he wanted to begin his courtship of Miss Dobson before anyone else was in the field.

Miss Lomas opened the door. She paled slightly as she saw William.

"You're rather early," she said.

"Yes, I thought I'd come early so's to be sure to be in time," said William. "Which room're we goin' to have tea in?"

With a gesture of hopelessness Miss Lomas showed him into the empty drawing-room.

"It's Miss Dobson I've really come for," explained William obligingly as he sat down.

Miss Lomas fled, but Miss Dobson did not appear.

William spent the interval wrestling with his Valentine. He had carried it sticky side towards his coat, and it now adhered closely to him.

He managed at last to tear it away, leaving a good deal of glue and bits of yew-tree still attached to the coat . . .

The guests began to arrive, Robert and Ethel among the first. Miss Dobson came in with Robert. He handed her a large box of chocolates.

"A Valentine," he said.

"Oh . . . thank you," said Miss Dobson, blushing.

William took up his enormous piece of gluey cardboard with bits of battered yew adhering at intervals.

"A Valentine," he said.

Miss Dobson looked at it in silence.

"W-what is it, William?" she said faintly.

"A Valentine," repeated William, annoyed at its reception.

"Oh," said Miss Dobson.

Robert led her over to the recess by the window, which contained two chairs. William followed, carrying his chair. He sat down beside them. Both ignored him.

"Quite a nice day, isn't it?" said Robert.

"Isn't it!" said Miss Dobson.

"Miss Dobson," said William, "I'm always dreamin' of you when I'm awake."

"What a pretty idea of yours to have a Valentine's Day party," said Robert.

"Do you think so?" said Miss Dobson coyly.

"Has anyone ever told you that you're like a bottled cherry?" said William doggedly.

"Do you know . . . this is the first Valentine I've ever given anyone?" said Robert.

"Oh . . . is it?" she said.

"I've been thinkin' about love at first sight," said William monotonously. "I got such a fright when I saw you first. I think we're pre-existed for each other. I—"

"Will you allow me to take you out in my side-car tomorrow?" said Robert.

"Oh, how lovely!" said Miss Dobson.

"No . . . predestinated . . . that's it," said William.

Neither of them took any notice of him. He felt depressed, and disillusioned. She wasn't much of a catch anyway. He didn't know why he'd even bothered about her.

He was quiet for a minute or two. Then he took up his Valentine which was lying on the floor, and walked out.

The Outlaws were in the old barn. They greeted William joyfully. Joan, the only girl member, was there with them. William handed her his cardboard.

"A Valentine," he said.

"A Valentine?" said Joan.

"Yes. Some say it's a saint what wrote soppy letters to girls an' some say it's a bit of fern like this an' some say it's a box of chocolates."

"Well, I never!" said Joan. "It's beautiful of you to give it to me, William."

76

"It's a jolly good piece of cardboard," said Ginger. "'F we scrape away these messy leaves an' stuff."

William joined with zest in the scraping.

"How's Albert?" said Joan.

After all, there was no one quite like Joan. He'd never contemplate marrying anyone else again.

"He's been took off me," said William.

"Oh, what a *shame*, William!"

"But I've got another . . . an earwig . . . called Fred."

"I'm so glad."

"But I like you better than *any* insect, Joan," he said generously.

"Oh, William, do you *really*?"

"Yes – an' I'm goin' to marry you when I grow up if you won't want me to talk a lot of soppy stuff that no one can understand."

"Oh, thank you, William . . . No, I won't."

"All right . . . now come on an' let's play Red Indians."

WILLIAM AND THE PRIZE CAT

& OTHER STORIES

Contents

William and the Prize Cat   83

William's April Fool's Day   103

William and the Twins   121

Revenge is Sweet   143

William and the Prize Cat

William and Ginger ambled slowly down the lane. Henry and Douglas had succumbed to a local epidemic of mumps, and so William and Ginger were the only two representatives of the Outlaws at large.

Suddenly, round a bend in the roadway, they ran into the Hubert Laneites, their rivals and enemies from time immemorial.

Hubert Lane, standing in the centre of his little band, smiled fatly at them.

"Hello," he said. "Been to the circus?"

Hubert Lane had a knack of finding out most things about his enemies, and he was well aware that the Outlaws had *not* been to the circus, because they had not enough money for their entrance fee.

"Circus?" said William carelessly. "Oh, what circus?"

"Why, the one over at Little Marleigh," said Hubert, slightly deflated.

"Oh, *that* one," said William, smiling. "Oh, you mean that one. It's not much of a circus, is it?"

Hubert Lane had recourse to heavy sarcasm.

"Oh no. It takes a much grander circus than that to satisfy you, I suppose."

"Well," said William mysteriously, "I know a jolly sight more about circuses then *most* people."

The Hubert Laneites laughed mockingly.

"How do you know more about circuses then most people?" challenged Hubert.

William considered this in silence for a moment, then said, still more mysteriously, "Wouldn't you like to know?"

Hubert eyed him uncertainly. He suspected that William's deep mysteriousness was bluff, and yet he was half impressed by it.

"All right," he said. "You prove it. I'll believe it when you prove it."

"All right," retorted William. "You jolly well wait and see."

Hubert sniggered, but for the present he turned to another subject.

"I'm getting up a cat show this afternoon," he said innocently. "There's a big box of

85

chocolates for the prize. Would you like to bring your cat along?"

The brazen shamelessness of this for a minute took away William's breath.

It was well known that Hubert's mother possessed a cat of gigantic proportions which had won many prizes at shows.

That the Hubert Laneites should try to win public prestige for themselves and secure their own box of chocolates by organising a cat show, was a piece of impudence worthy of them.

"Like to enter your cat?" repeated Hubert carelessly.

William thought of the scrawny creature which represented the sole feline staff of his household.

Hubert thought of it too.

"I suppose it wouldn't have much of a chance," said Hubert at last, with nauseating pity in his voice.

"It would. It's a jolly fine cat," said William indignantly.

"Want to enter it then?" said Hubert, satisfied with the cunning that had made William thus court public humiliation.

The Browns' cat was the worst-looking cat in the village.

"All right," he said. "I'll put you down. Bring it along this afternoon."

William and Ginger walked dejectedly away.

Early that afternoon they set off, William carefully carrying the Browns' cat, brushed till it was in a state bordering on madness, and adorned with a blue bow taken off a boudoir cap of his sister, Ethel, at which it tore furiously in the intervals of scratching William.

"Well, it's got spirit anyway," said William proudly. "And that ought to count. It's got more spirit then that fat ole thing of Hubert's mother's."

As if to corroborate his statement the cat shot out a paw and gave him a scratch from forehead to chin, then leapt from his arms and fled down the road still tearing madly at its blue bow.

"There," said Ginger. "Now you've gone and done it. Now we've got to go without a cat or not go at all."

William considered these alternatives gloomily. "Mmm. An' they'll go on and on, 'cause they know we can't go to the circus," he added.

"Well, what shall we do?" said Ginger.

"Let's sit down and wait a bit," said William, "and try 'n' think of a plan. We might find a stray cat bigger 'n theirs. Let's just sit down and think."

Ginger shook his head at William's optimism.

They were sitting down on the roadside, their backs to the wood that bordered the road. William turned to look into the wood.

"There's wild cats anyway," he said. "I bet there's still a few wild cats left in England. I bet *they're* bigger than his mother's ole cat. I shun't be a bit surprised if there were some wild cats left in this wood. I'm goin' to have a look anyway."

And he was just going to make his way through the hedge, when the most amazing thing happened.

Out of the wood, gambolling playfully, came a gigantic – was it a cat? It was certainly near enough to a cat to be called a cat. But it was far from wild.

It greeted Ginger and William affectionately, rolling over on to its back and offering
itself to be stroked and rubbed.

They stared at it in amazement.

"It's a wild cat," said William. "A tame
wild cat. P'raps hunger made it tame. P'raps
it's the last wild cat left in England. Puss! Puss!
Puss!"

It leapt upon him affectionately.

"It's a *jolly* fine wild cat," he said, stroking
it, "and we're jolly lucky to have found a cat
like this. Look at it. It knows it belongs to us
now."

"We'd better take it to the show," said
Ginger. "It's nearly time."

So they made a collar for it by tying
Ginger's tie loosely round its neck, and a lead
by taking a bootlace out of William's boot and
attaching it to the tie, and set off towards the
Lanes' house.

The other competitors were all there,
holding more or less unwilling exhibits, and
in the place of honour was Hubert Lane

holding his mother's enormous tabby.

But the Lane tabby was a kitten compared with William's wild cat.

The assembled competitors stared at it speechlessly as William, with a nonchalant air, took his seat with it, amongst them.

"That – that's not a cat," gasped Hubert Lane.

William had with difficulty gathered his exhibit upon his knee. He challenged them round its head.

"What is it then?" he said.

They had no answer. It was certainly more like a cat than anything.

"'Course it's a cat," said William, pursuing his advantage.

"Well, whose is it then?" said Hubert indignantly. "I bet it's not yours."

"It *is* mine," said William.

"Well, why have we never seen it before then?" said Hubert.

"D'you think," said William, "do you think we'd let a valubul cat like this run about all over the place? Let me tell you, this is a 'specially famous cat, that never comes out except to go to shows, and that's won prizes all over the world. Well, I've not got much time. I've gotter get back home. So if our cat's bigger 'n yours you'd better give me the prize now. This cat's not used to bein' kept hangin' about before bein' given its prize."

The Hubert Laneites sagged visibly gazing at the monster which sat calmly on William's knees, rubbing its face against his neck affectionately.

Hubert Lane knew when he had met defeat. He took the large box of chocolates on which the Hubert Laneites had meant to feast that afternoon and, still gaping at the prizewinner, handed it to William.

The other exhibitors cheered. William put the box of chocolates under his arm, and set off leading his exhibit.

It was not till they reached the gate that the Hubert Laneites recovered from their

stupefaction and yelled as with one accord, "Who can't afford to go the circus? *Yah!*"

William was still drunk with the pride of possession.

"It's a jolly fine wild cat," he said again.

"Where'll we keep it?" said Ginger practically.

"In the old barn," said William, "an' we'll not tell anyone about it. We'll keep it there an' take it out for walks in the wood an' bring it food from home to eat. Then I vote we send it in for some real cat shows. I bet it'll win a lot of money. I bet it'll make us millionaires. An' when I'm a millionaire I'm going to buy a circus with every sort of animal in the world in it."

The mention of the circus rather depressed them. And Ginger, to cheer them up, suggested eating the chocolates.

They descended into the ditch and sat there with the prize cat between them.

It seemed that the prize cat, too, liked chocolates and the three of them shared them equally till the box was finished.

"Well it's had its tea now," said Ginger, "so let's take it straight to the old barn for the night."

"You don't know that it's had enough," said William. "It might want a bit of something else. We'll take it to the old barn, then you go home and get some food for it."

"All right," said Ginger. "I'll bring it what I can find with no one catchin' me. It'll depend whether the larder window's open."

Ginger departed and William amused himself by playing with his prize cat. It was an excellent playfellow.

It made little feints and darts at William. It rolled over on the ground. It growled and pretended to fight him. The time passed on wings until Ginger returned.

Ginger's arms were full. Evidently the larder window *had* been open.

He was carrying two buns, half an apple pie and a piece of cheese, and yet despite this rich haul his expression was one of deepest melancholy.

He placed the things absently down upon a packing case and said, "I met a boy in the road, and he'd just met a man, and he said they were looking for a lion cub that had got away from the circus."

William's face dropped. They both gazed thoughtfully at the prize cat.

"I – I sort of thought it was a lion cub all the time," said William

"So did I," said Ginger hastily.

After a long silence, William said, "Well, I suppose we've gotter take it back."

He spoke as one whose world had crashed about him. Life without the lion cub stretched grey and dark before him, hardly worth living.

"I s'pose we've gotter," said Ginger. "I s'pose it's stealin' if we don't. Now that we know."

They placed the food before the cub and watched it with melancholy tenderness.

It ate the buns, sat on the apple pie, and played football with the piece of cheese.

Then they took up the end of William's bootlace again and set off sorrowfully with it to Little Marleigh.

The proprietor of the circus received the truant with relief and complimented the rescuers on its prompt return.

They gazed at it sadly, Ginger replacing his tie, and William his bootlace.

"He's a cute little piece, isn't he?" said the

proprietor. "Don't appear yet. Too young. But goin' to lap up tricks like milk soon. Well I'd better be getting a move on. Early show's jus' goin' to begin. Thank you, young sirs."

"I s'pose," said William wistfully, "I s'pose we couldn't *do* anything in the show?"

The proprietor scratched his head.

"I tell you what. I am short-handed as it happens. I could do with another hand. Just movin' things off an' on between turns. Care to help with that?"

So deep was their emotion, that William broke his bootlace and Ginger nearly throttled himself with his tie.

"I should – jolly well – think – we would," said William.

The Hubert Laneites sat together in the front row. They'd all been to the circus earlier in the week, but they'd come again for this last performance partly in order to be able to tell the Outlaws that they'd been twice, and partly to comfort themselves for the fiasco of their cat show.

"I say," said Hubert Lane to Bertie Franks, "I say, won't old William be mad when we tell him we've been again."

"Yeah," said Bertie Franks. "Yeah. And I say, fancy him havin' the cheek to say he knew more about circuses than us and not even been once. We won't half rag him about it. We won't . . ."

His voice died away. He stared down into the ring. For there unmistakably was William, setting out the little tubs on which the performing ponies performed.

He rubbed his eyes and looked again. It *was* William.

"*Golly*," he said faintly.

All the Hubert Laneites were staring at William, paralysed with amazement.

"*Golly*," they echoed and drew another deep breath as Ginger appeared carrying the chairs on which the clown pretended to do acrobatic feats.

Then the circus began. The Hubert Laneites did not see the circus at all. They were staring fascinated at the opening of the tent into which William and Ginger had vanished.

After the first turn they emerged and moved away the little tubs and brought out a lot of letters, which they laid on the ground for the talking horse to spell from.

After that turn, William came out alone and held a hoop for Nellie the Wonder Dog to jump through.

Not once did the expressions of stupefied amazement fade from the faces of the Hubert Laneites.

The next day they approached William with something of reverence in their expressions.

"I say, William," Hubert said humbly. "Tell us about it, will you?"

"About what?" said William.

"About you helpin' at the circus."

"Oh, *that*," said William carelessly. "Oh I gen'rally help at circuses round about here. I don't always go into the ring, like what I did yesterday, but I'm gen'rally in the tent behind helpin' with the animals, trainin' 'em for their tricks, getting 'em ready and such like. I said I knew a jolly sight more about circuses than what you did, you remember?"

"Yes," said Hubert Lane still more humbly. "It must be jolly fun, isn't it, William?"

"Oh, it's all right," said William. "It's hard

work, and of course it's jolly dangerous. Trainin' the animals and lockin' 'em up for the night and such like."

He walked a few hundred yards with an ostentatious limp, and then said, "The elephant trod on my foot yesterday when I was puttin' it in its cage."

He touched the scratch that his mother's cat had made.

"The bear gave me this the other night, when I was combin' it out ready to go on and do its tricks. It's work not everyone would like to do."

They gazed at him as at a being from another and a higher sphere.

"I say, William," said Bertie Franks. "If – er – if – they want anyone else to help you, you'll give us a chance, won't you?"

"I don't s'pose they will," said William. "'Sides, this circus has gone now and I don't know when another's comin'. It's dangerous work, you know, but I'm used to it."

And, followed by their admiring eyes, he limped elaborately away. He was limping with the other foot this time. But of course, no one noticed that.

William's April Fool's Day

April the First was a day generally enjoyed to the full by William, but this year something seemed to have gone wrong.

Not one of his efforts had been successful.

Ethel had calmly put on one side, without even attempting to crack it, the empty eggshell that he had carefully arranged in her egg-cup.

Robert had removed the upturned tin-tack from his chair before sitting down, and had placed it so neatly upon William's that William had been taken unawares.

His father had refused even to raise his eyes from his newspaper at William's excited

shout, "Look, Father, there's a cow in the garden."

And his mother had merely murmured, "Yes, dear" when William had informed her that Ethel had been bitten by a mad dog on her way to the village.

His attempts to make April Fools of his Outlaws had been no more successful. They were all, indeed, so much upon their guard that none of them would answer the simplest question or pay heed to the most innocent remark.

At last, they abandoned hostilities and formed an offensive alliance against the other boys of the neighbourhood.

But not even this was successful. The other boys of the neighbourhood, also, were too well up in the rules of the game to be taken in by the well-worn tricks the Outlaws played on them.

Advised of the near approach of bulls, runaway horses, motor cars out of control, they merely made faces at the Outlaws.

Informed that sweets were being given away at Mr Moss's sweet shop, that a circus had just arrived at the other end of the village, that Farmer Jenks was riding round his farmyard on his old sow, they merely remarked, "Yah! April Fool yourself!"

"I wish we could find someone that had forgotten it was April Fool's Day," said Henry.

"Tell you what I'd like to do," said William dreamily. "I'd like to make someone really important an April Fool. Let's think who's the most important person living here."

"The Vicar?" suggested Ginger.

"The doctor?" suggested Douglas.

"Yes, I think the doctor," said William. "He'd be easier to make one, anyway . . . I know! I've thought of something to bring them *both* in."

Followed by his Outlaws, William made his way up to the doctor's front door, knocked at it smartly and informed the maid who opened it that the Vicar was dying and would the doctor please go to him at once.

For answer he received a box on the ear that nearly made him lose his balance.

He rejoined his friends, rubbing his boxed ear tenderly and filled with righteous indignation.

"Huh! S'pose it was true an' they'd let the poor Vicar die. Well, I think she's the same as a murderer, that woman is. I've a good mind to go an' *tell* the Vicar that she's as good as murdered him. I bet I was as near dead as you could be too, with a bang like that on the side of my head. She oughter get put in prison for murdering both of us. I'm jolly well sick of April Fool's Day, anyway. I vote we go and play somewhere . . ."

It was decided that it would be hardly safe to play in their own village. Their own village was too full of their enemies, eager to use the noble festival of All Fools' Day as an opportunity of getting even with them.

They could not safely relax their guard for a moment in their own village.

"Let's go over to Marleigh," suggested Ginger, "an' take the football with us."

The Outlaws were comparatively unknown in Marleigh.

"Good," agreed William. "We'll get a bit of peace there."

They set off briskly across the fields to Marleigh and there found a vacant plot of land on which to hold a football match.

"A beastly house next to it, of course," said William morosely, "and they'll be sure to make a beastly fuss every time the ball goes into the garden. I don't think there's a single place left to play in England that hasn't got a house next to it, all ready to make a fuss the minute your ball goes into its garden. Sometimes I feel I don't care how soon the end of the world comes."

"Well, come on, let's begin to play," said Ginger.

They began to play and, in a few minutes, as William had prophesied, their ball went over the wall into the garden of the house.

It was a high brick wall with no convenient

foothold on it, so they went to the gate to survey the enemy's ground.

There they found that to get round to the side garden where their ball was, they would have to pass a window where a haughty-looking lady sat at a writing-table. Clearly it could not be done.

"We'll have to go to the door and ask," said William cheerfully. (William's spirits always rose at a crisis.) "I'll put on my polite look."

William's polite look, though much admired by himself and his friends, was in reality a sickly leer.

It certainly did not seem to ingratiate him with the housemaid who opened the door.

"Please can we go round to your garden to get our ball, if you don't mind, thank you very much?"

The housemaid stared at him disapprovingly, disappeared, and soon returned to say shortly, "She says it's an intolerable nuisance, but you can this once."

"Thank you very much," said William,

widening his leer and making her a courtly bow.

"None of your impudence!" she said, and slammed the door in his face.

The Outlaws went round to the side of the house and found the ball.

They returned to the plot of waste land and continued their interrupted match.

In five minutes the ball had gone over the wall again. They considered the situation with some dismay.

"I'm not going to ask again," said William firmly. "She'll start murdering me same as the other one did if I go. You'd better go, Ginger."

"All right," said Ginger and began to compose his features into an imitation of William's leer as he walked up to the front door.

The same housemaid opened it, received Ginger's dulcet request with obvious indignation, then retired to report it to her mistress.

She returned almost immediately.

"She says you ought to be ashamed of

yourselves pestering like this. She says you can get it this once, but she says she'll send for the police if it goes on."

Ginger retrieved the ball and rejoined his friends.

"Gosh!" he said. "More like dragons than yuman bein's round here, aren't they? We'll take jolly good care not to let it go over again, anyway."

They returned to their game but five minutes later an energetic and unguarded kick from Douglas sent the ball once more into the forbidden garden.

"Well, it's you or Henry to get it now," said William. "Me an' Ginger's had our turns."

"They all look pretty savage about here," said Douglas. "They look as if they'd kill you as soon as look at you. I votes we go home an' leave it."

"Yes, I dare say you do," said William. "It's not your football. It's my football, an' I'm not goin' home without it, so there!"

"What are you goin' to do then?"

"I'm goin' to get it. I'm goin' to crawl round to the garden on my hands and knees, so's she can't see me from the window, an' get it."

"I'll come with you," said Ginger.

"So will I," said Douglas and Henry.

There was no need for more than one to go to fetch the ball, but when there was any danger the Outlaws liked to face it together.

In single file, on hands and knees, they made their way to the garden and retrieved the ball.

In single file, on hands and knees, they began their journey back.

But, just as they were passing beneath the window, Ginger sneezed, and the amazed and indignant face of the lady of the house appeared in the window, disappeared, then reappeared now more indignant than amazed at the door.

The Outlaws rose sheepishly to their feet.

The lady stood barring their path and giving eloquent voice to her indignation.

"Disgraceful . . . *disgraceful*! I've a good mind to send for the police and have you charged for trespassing. If I ever see any of you inside this garden again, I'll send for the police at *once* . . . Go away this *minute*. If I knew who your parents were, I'd write to them most strongly."

The Outlaws fled, William clutching his beloved football.

"Well, it's time to go home, anyway," he said.

"Yes, it's nearly twelve," said Ginger,

pretending to consult his watch (which never went for more than five minutes) but in reality glancing at the church clock that showed above the trees.

"Nearly twelve," said William wistfully, "and we've not made anyone an April Fool. It'll be the first year I ever remember that we've not made anyone an April Fool."

"We've not been made one ourselves, anyway," Ginger reminded him.

"Huh – 'course not!" said William scornfully. "Catch anyone makin' April Fools of *us*! That's not the point. The point is that we've not made anyone one. It seems awful somehow not to have made anyone an April Fool on April Fool's Day."

"Well, it's not quite twelve yet," said Ginger. "It's not too late."

"Yes, but who is there to make one here?" said William.

At that moment a boy was seen coming towards them.

He was fat and pale, and he looked both

stupid and conceited. The Outlaws took an immediate dislike to him.

"Let's make *him* one," whispered William.

"Yes, but *how*?" said Ginger.

"I know!" said William.

The boy had come abreast of them now. He gave them a challenging grimace.

"I say," said William with well-assumed friendliness, "what do you like best? What sort of cakes, I mean?"

"Coconut buns," answered the boy promptly.

William gave a short surprised laugh.

"Well, that's a funny thing."

He pointed to the house that had been the scene of their escapade.

"You see that house?"

"Yes," said the boy.

"Well, the lady that lives there, she always gives coconut buns to any boys who come to ask if they can get their ball from her garden. If you want some coconut buns all you have to do is go up to the door and knock and ask

if you can speak to the mistress of the house. And when you get to her, all you've got to say is that you're one of the boys who've been playing ball just outside her garden this morning, and the ball's gone over again, and may you fetch it. And when you've said that, she'll give you some coconut buns."

The boy stared at them.

"Go on," William urged him, glancing at the clock, and seeing the fingers perilously near the fatal hour.

"Go on. We *want* you to have those buns 'cause – you look hungry. See here . . ." desperately he took a treasured whistle from his pocket, "I'll give you that if you'll go an' say it."

The boy took and pocketed it without a word.

William's urgency communicated itself to the others.

They felt that their very honour depended upon somehow or other making this boy an April Fool before twelve o'clock.

"And look here," said Ginger feverishly. "I'll give you this penknife, too, if you'll go quick. We – we *want* you to have those coconut buns."

The boy pocketed the penknife, too, stared at them for another moment, then said, "All right" and, walking up to the front door, rang the bell.

The housemaid opened it and he was admitted. The door closed. The Outlaws danced a silent dance of triumph and delight at the gate.

Then they waited impatiently for the fleeing form of their victim to issue, pursued by the wrath of the redoubtable lady of the house.

Nothing happened.

"Perhaps she's rung up the police," said William, looking anxiously down the road.

"Well, if she has, we've made April Fools of them," said Ginger triumphantly.

"I – I hope she's not murderin' him," said Douglas. "We shall get into a beastly row if we've got him murdered."

But at that moment an upstairs window was flung open, and the boy appeared at it.

He held a coconut bun in one hand, the whistle and penknife in the other.

He grinned and munched and waved his spoils at them exultantly.

"W-w-w-what are you doing there?" stammered William.

"I live here," shouted the boy. "It's my home. Yah-boo! April Fools!"

He laid down the coconut bun and took up a pea-shooter.

The clock from the church tower struck twelve.

"April Fools!" called the boy again.

The Outlaws turned and began to walk slowly down the road.

A pea caught William neatly just above one ear.

William and the Twins

Honeysuckle Cottage stood empty and William (who took a great interest in Honeysuckle Cottage) always made a short detour on his way home from school in order to see if there were any signs of new inhabitants.

His joy therefore was great when, one evening, he saw unmistakable signs of occupation, all the windows open, and an easel standing in the little garden. An Artist.

Next morning he was up early and made his way to Honeysuckle Cottage. He crept cautiously up the path and peered in at the open kitchen door.

And there he stood motionless, for a most extraordinary couple were engaged upon preparations for breakfast.

Both had exactly the same face – pale and narrow, framed in short, lank, fair hair.

Both wore white silk shirts and coats of homespun tweeds.

That one was a man and the other a woman was evident from the fact that one wore knickerbockers and the other a skirt. Beneath these garments they wore worsted stockings and brogues.

Both were leaning over the gas stove, the man anxiously watching a saucepan of six eggs, the woman making coffee.

The woman turned round suddenly, and saw William standing in the open doorway.

"Watch this and see that it doesn't boil," she said to him casually, "or else take those plates into the dining-room."

"I'll take the plates," said William, thrilled at being thus accepted as a member of the party. He carried the plates into the dining-room. "These eggs are done, I should think."

"Have I done too many? I just put in all the man brought."

"Oh no," said William reassuringly. "I don't think they're too many."

The man seemed cheered. "No, I suppose there aren't."

The woman came in with the coffee, and he pointed to her, to William, and to himself.

"No, of course, just two each, isn't it? That's not too many."

William sat down. The woman passed him a cup of coffee, the man gave him two eggs, and the meal began. The strange couple accepted him without question.

Suddenly the woman looked at him and said, "Why aren't you drinking your coffee?"

"I never drink coffee," said William. "I don't like it."

She looked at the man and sighed. "He's right, you know," she said. "One shouldn't

drink stimulants of any sort if one wants to keep the psychic faculties unclouded."

She turned to William again. "What do you drink?"

"I drink liqu'rice water mostly," said William.

"Liquorice water," she said vaguely. "I must try it."

William, who had finished his eggs, murmured something about going home to breakfast.

He departed quietly homeward, where he made an excellent breakfast of porridge, scrambled eggs, toast, butter and marmalade.

After school he made his way at once to Honeysuckle Cottage.

The man was seated at an easel in the little orchard, and the woman in a deck-chair on the little lawn.

She looked at William and said, "Do you see nature spirits?"

William stared at her in amazement.

"Children often do see them," went on the lady, "though my great friend Elissa Freedom – you may have heard of her, she's well known in the psychic world – says that she didn't see them as a child, though she sees them now quite plainly. I really must show you some of her photographs. She has a lovely one of a birch tree with the outline of a nature spirit standing near it. About the size of a child . . . faint, you know, but quite unmistakable. She says that everything in nature has its attendant spirit. Of the same colour generally. I've brought a camera with me, but so far I haven't had any success."

"Uh-huh," agreed William, completely mystified.

"That, of course, is why Tristram and I have come here," she went on. "Tristram is my twin brother. We want to cultivate our psychic faculties. My brother will – er – surrender himself to psychic influences in the hope of doing inspirational painting, and I am going to try to cultivate my psychic vision till I can see a nature spirit. I take it that you are interested in the psychic side of life?"

"Uh-huh," agreed William again.

"Have you had any experiences?"

"Me?" said William. "Oh yes, lots."

But before he could tell her any of his favourite imaginary exploits, the church clock struck five, and she rose slowly from her deck-chair.

"It's tea-time, I suppose," she said. "Of course, one shouldn't really drink stimulants when one's trying to acquire psychic vision."

As they entered the kitchen, she turned suddenly to William.

"What did you say you drank?"

"Me?" said William. "Liqu'rice water mostly."

"Liquorice water? I don't think I've ever tasted it. Where do you get it?"

"I make it," said William modestly.

He pulled a bottle out of his pocket and with an air of great gallantry poured some into a saucer for her to drink.

She tasted it with a critical frown. The frown vanished.

"It's very nice," she said. "A pure herbal drink, of course."

"Uh-huh," said William.

"You must show me how to make it," she said.

William was thrilled. He'd never before met a grown-up who did not look upon liquorice water as a messy juvenile concoction to be thrown away whenever discovered.

Tristram came in from his easel in the

orchard. His sister poured him a saucer of the liquorice water.

"I thought, Tristram," she said, "that during this retirement from the world we should give up stimulants. They dull the psychic faculties, you know, so we're having liquorice water."

Tristram tasted it.

"Delicious," he said. "Quite delicious."

"The boy made it," said his sister, "but I dare say the stores could get it for us. The boy always drinks liquorice water and he says that he has had psychic experiences."

William had come to the conclusion that "psychic" was a synonym for "exciting".

The woman said, "Have you had any success, Tristram?"

"N-not exactly," he confessed. "I – surrender myself and try to paint what comes into my head, as it were, but I can't help realising that it isn't as good as the work in which I *don't* surrender myself . . ."

The activities of the sister (whose name, William had discovered, was Miss Auriole Mannister) were not *very* exciting.

She sat gazing wistfully about the little garden, her camera poised for action upon whatever nature spirit should appear to her.

She asked William to leave the garden undisturbed to her between four and five o'clock, explaining that she thought that her psychic functions were most active then.

But William was finding the artist in the orchard even more interesting than the vision-seeker in the garden.

The artist sat before his easel with a palette in his hand, executing on his canvas a series of amazing strokes that reminded William of the nightmare he had had after last year's November the Fifth's firework display.

The artist noticed William's expression and said in his gentle, melancholy voice, "It's not meant to represent what one sees, you know. It's meant to represent the emotions the sight of it rouses in one."

"Yes," said William, trying to sound as if he understood.

William hadn't realised that painting pictures – real pictures – was *quite* as easy as that, simply splodging paint about anyhow. It simplified the art considerably.

He surreptitiously tore pages out of his exercise books at school, and took them to the cottage with him.

There, he "borrowed" paint very cautiously, till he found that the artist took the situation as a matter of course.

If William happened to be using the paint

tube he wanted, he would wait quite patiently till William had finished with it.

Gradually, William came to look upon himself as an accomplished artist.

He boasted of his skill to his friends till Ginger said, "All right, paint us something then, an' let's see."

"All right, I will," said William. "What'll I paint you?"

"Paint us a sign to put up at the ole barn."

"All right. What'll I paint on it?"

"A lion."

William began his lion that evening. Tristram was working indoors in water colours. Both of them set to work, side by side.

Once, Miss Auriole looked in and whispered, "How are you getting on, Tristram?" and Tristram said, "I'm surrendering myself *utterly*, but I don't know what the results will be."

"I *do* hope it will be all right," said his sister, and added, "I'm waiting and watching with my camera outside."

William finished his lion. He considered it an excellent lion. It looked as spirited and ferocious as a lion ought to look.

He went outside to look at Miss Auriole. She was asleep in a deck-chair with her camera on her knee.

Then he went home and didn't realise till he was in bed that he'd left his lion behind in the little studio.

After school next day, William took Ginger

round to the cottage. They entered the garden cautiously, and crept towards the study window.

"My painting's in here," William said, then he stopped.

Through the study window he could see his two friends and a strange man with a beard standing round the little desk.

He retreated.

"We'll wait till they come out," he said.

"Let's have a game of Hide and Seek," said Ginger.

"All right. I'll hide. You count."

"One . . . two . . . three . . ."

William crept down to the bottom of the lawn where the heap of grass cuttings stood, and with a dexterous movement inserted himself into the very middle of it.

Soon he heard Ginger shout "Com—" and stop suddenly.

Then he heard the sounds of the lady setting up her deck-chair on the lawn.

William remained in his grass heap

wondering what to do. It was the hour during which the lady had asked him to leave her undisturbed.

For a moment he considered remaining where he was, till the end of the hour, but he was already tired of swallowing grass cuttings.

If he waited just a few minutes, it would be all right; she'd be fast asleep.

He waited till he imagined that he heard deep breathing, then rose from the heap, fled behind the greenhouse and out through a hole in the hedge.

Simultaneous sounds of a gasp and a click pursued him. Scattering grass cuttings at every step, he hastened down to the road.

He eventually found Ginger hanging about the gate of the cottage.

"Hello!" he greeted William. "I had to go 'cause she came out. Where were you hidin'?"

"In the grass."

"Well, let's try 'n' get your paintin' now."

They entered the little garden again.

Tristram was just joining his sister on the lawn.

"Tristram!" she greeted him excitedly. "I've seen one. Oh, my dear! It was so thrilling. I was sitting here as usual with my camera, watching and waiting, when suddenly, from that grass heap, there detached itself a faint green wraith – a shadowy spirit. For one second I saw it standing by the heap as plainly as I see you now, and then it disappeared."

"You got a snap of it, I hope," said Tristram anxiously.

"Yes, my dear. Oh, I hope so. If what I saw comes out, I can die happy. And what about your paintings, my dear?"

Tristram's face clouded over.

"It's no good. Tosher says that none of them will do for the journal. He says that they aren't *inspirational enough*."

"Oh, *Tristram*! I'm so sorry. Where is he? Has he gone?"

"No, he's still in the study. His train doesn't go till half-past."

"Let's go out for a walk, dear. It will do you good. He won't mind being left till his train goes, I'm sure."

Together the twins set off for their walk. Together Ginger and William crept round to the little studio, but the man with the beard was still there.

"I can't get it now," said William.

"I don't b'lieve you ever did it," said Ginger.

"All right," said William, "you wait till tomorrow."

Tomorrow came, and William went into the little studio, but he couldn't find his lion painting.

Ginger spent a pleasant day jeering at him, and then they both completely forgot the incident.

There were all the signs of departure at Honeysuckle Cottage. Boxes stood packed on the doorstep. The decrepit village taxi was at the little gate.

William hung about disconsolately. He was sorry to say goodbye to his friends. Suddenly he saw the postman at the gate, and he went down to get the letters.

There were two bulky packets – one for Tristram, and one for his sister.

Auriole fell upon hers with a cry of joy, and unwrapped half a dozen papers bearing the inscription *Psychic Realm*.

"My photograph!" she said, turning over

the pages with trembling fingers. Then she gave a scream of excitement.

"Here it is! Look!"

William and Tristram looked.

There was a photograph of the grass heap at the end of the lawn and, by it, the grass-covered figure of William, preparing to creep furtively away.

Beneath it was the legend: "Nature Spirit, photographed by Miss Auriole Mannister".

William gaped at it, speechless with amazement.

Before he could say anything, however, Tristram, too, had uttered a cry of surprise and excitement. He too had unwrapped half a dozen copies of *Psychic Realm* and had a letter in his hand.

"Listen," he said, "it's from Tosher. He says, 'After you'd gone I found a really splendid bit of inspirational painting in your studio. Why didn't you show it to me? It's truly inspired. I have called it *Vision* and it's reproduced on page 26.'"

Both of them turned over the pages frenziedly. "Here it is! Look!"

And there was William's lion, and underneath the words, "*Vision*: inspirational painting by Mr Tristram Mannister".

"But do you know," said Tristram in an awestruck voice, "I haven't the slightest memory of ever doing it."

"You must have done it in a state of ecstasy, dear," said Miss Auriole reverently.

"I must," said Tristram. "It's – it's the most wonderful thing that's ever happened to me."

Then the cab driver called to them saying that, blimey, they'd miss it if they didn't hurry, and they had gone before William recovered the power of speech.

They had, however, left a copy of *Psychic Realm* behind them, and William, with mingled feelings of pride and bewilderment, picked it up and put it in his pocket.

He showed the two pictures to everyone he knew, pointing out that the Nature Spirit

was himself, and that he had executed the inspirational painting of *Vision*.

No one, of course, believed him.

Revenge is Sweet

The Outlaws were agog with excitement, for the day of Hubert Lane's party was drawing near. This may sound as though the Outlaws were to be honoured guests at Hubert's party.

Far from it.

For between the Outlaws and the Hubert Laneites a deadly feud waged, and tradition demanded that they should treat each other's parties with indifference.

It was the Hubert Laneites who had broken that tradition. They had deliberately wrecked William's party the week before.

They had substituted a deceased cat for the

rabbit which the conjuror had brought with him and which was to appear miraculously from his hat.

The Outlaws were now out for revenge.

They were determined to wreck Hubert Lane's party, as Hubert Lane had wrecked theirs.

The news that Mr and Mrs Lane would be away for the party and that Hubert's Aunt Emmy would preside heartened the Outlaws considerably.

The Outlaws had met Aunt Emmy. Anything vaguer, kinder, more short-sighted, and more well-meaning than Aunt Emmy, could scarcely be imagined.

The Outlaws had made no definite plans. William, like all the best generals, preferred not to draw up his own plan of action till he had ascertained the enemy's.

The party was to begin at seven. At half-past six, ten boys in single file might have been observed creeping through a hole in the fence that bordered the Lane garden.

At the head crept William, his freckled face contorted into a scowl expressive of determination to do or die.

Behind him came Ginger, behind him Henry, behind him Douglas, and behind Douglas came six anti-Laneites and supporters of the Outlaws.

A pear tree grew conveniently up the side of the Lane mansion . . .

Hubert was in his bedroom at the other side of the house, anxiously arraying himself in an Eton suit and shining pumps.

The maids were in the kitchen giving the final touches to mountains of sandwiches and trifles and cakes and jellies and blancmanges.

Mr and Mrs Lane were away at the bedside of an exasperatingly healthy aged relative, and Aunt Emmy was in the kitchen driving the maids to distraction by her well-meant efforts to "help". She had already sprinkled salt over a trifle, under the impression that it was sugar.

So there was no one to oppose or even notice the Outlaws as, one by one, they

145

climbed up the perilous branches of the pear tree and in at an attic window.

They sat on the floor and looked at each other, collars and ties awry, jackets torn, knees scratched and dirty.

The Lane attics consisted of three fair-sized rooms, packed with boxes, water cisterns, spiders' webs and mysterious pipes.

On the tiny landing outside was a small window leading straight out on to the roof. It was a boyhood's paradise.

The eyes of the Outlaws gleamed as they explored it. Then William called the attention of his band to the immediate object of the expedition.

"We've gotter creep out an' see what's happ'nin' first of all," he said hoarsely, "an' then – an' then we'll think what to do."

Very creakingly, on tiptoe, the Outlaws crept out after him and hung over the banisters of the attic staircase. Aunt Emmy's voice, clear and flute-like, arose from the hall.

"*That's* right, Hubert darling. You look *very* nice, my cherub, very nice indeed. *Quite* a little man."

"Your hair's coming down, Auntie," said Hubert.

"Little boys mustn't make personal remarks, darling," said Aunt Emmy.

The Outlaws were listening with silent rapture to this. William was storing up every word of the conversation in his mind for future use.

Then came the sound of the front door bell.

"The first guest, darling," said Aunt Emmy. "I'll open the door and you'd better stand just there to receive them – remember to say 'How d'you do?' nicely."

Then came the sound of the arrival of Bertie Franks, the most odious of the Hubert Laneites next to Hubert himself.

Arrivals followed fast and furious after that.

The Hubert Laneites all bore a curious physical resemblance to Hubert, their leader. They were all pale and fat.

They rallied round Hubert chiefly because of his unlimited pocket-money; and, like Hubert, when anyone annoyed them, they told their fathers and their fathers wrote notes about it to the fathers of those who had annoyed them.

The guests changed into pumps and drifted into the drawing-room. A dismal, very-first-beginning-of-the-party-silence reigned.

"Now, what shall we play at first?" said Aunt Emmy, with overdone brightness. "Puss in the Corner?"

This suggestion was met with chilly silence.

"Hunt the Slipper?" went on Aunt Emmy, her brightness becoming almost hysterical. Silence again.

One of the guests took the matter into his own hands.

"What about a game of Hide and Seek?"

"Hide and Seek . . ." quavered Aunt Emmy. "That's rather a *rough* game, isn't it?"

They assured her that it wasn't, and drew lots for who should be "It". The Outlaws, craning necks and ears over the attic staircase, gathered that Hubert was "It".

The guests, led by Bertie Franks, swarmed upstairs in search of hiding places. They swarmed up to the first floor and the second floor and began to swarm up to the attic.

Devoid of initiative they simply followed Bertie Franks. The Outlaws withdrew hastily to their lair . . .

"Here's a little window," squeaked a

Hubert Laneite, tugging it open. "Let's go 'n' hide on the roof."

"No," said Bertie Franks earnestly. "'S dangerous. We don't want to go anywhere dangerous. We might hurt ourselves."

"And we don't want to do anythin' to get our best clothes dirty," said another Laneite.

They entered the attic opposite to the one where the Outlaws were concealed.

"We could all hide here," said a Laneite, "behind boxes and things."

"Ugh! It's rather dusty," said another Laneite with distaste.

"Never mind," said a third. "It's not for long."

"Ugh! There's spiders an' things," said a fourth disgustedly.

"Let's shut the door so's he won't see us," said Bertie Franks.

Someone shut the door and from within came sounds of the Laneites settling into hiding places, moving boxes, and uttering exclamations of disgust as they did so.

Very quietly William slipped across and turned the key in the lock. Evidently no one heard him.

"Coming!" yelled Hubert Lane from downstairs.

"Don't shout so, darling," said Aunt Emmy's flute-like voice. "Say it quietly. Little gentlemen never raise their voices."

Hubert Lane came slowly upstairs. Some instinct seemed to lead him straight up to the attic.

He stopped at the open window. His orderly mind knew that it should be shut. And it was open.

They must have gone out on to the roof.

After a moment's hesitation he squeezed out of the window and began to explore the recesses of the chimney pots.

Like a flash William, who was watching behind the door, streaked to the window, shut it and bolted it.

Hubert turned in dismay, and William had a vision of Hubert's fat pale face staring open-mouthed through the pane, before, with admirable presence of mind, he moved two large table leaves that stood near, to shut out the sight.

That disposed of Hubert.

There was no real danger. The window gave on to a stretch of flat roof, bounded by a parapet and there was no fear of the cautious Hubert venturing anywhere near it.

The Outlaws streamed out of their hiding

place to join their leader. It was evident that William had some plan.

"Come along," he said, "an' do jus' what I do."

They followed him trustfully on his bold course downstairs – right down to the hall where Aunt Emmy stood smiling painfully and pinning up her ever-descending hair.

Very faintly from upstairs from behind the barrier of window pane and table leaves there came to them an indignant, protesting "Hey!"

As to most of us hens are just hens, so to Aunt Emmy boys were just boys.

About ten boys had ascended the stairs and now about ten boys descended.

It did not occur to her that they might not be the same boys.

Even had she been less short-sighted, that possibility would not have occurred to her.

She did notice that their former spick and span appearance was somewhat blurred, but she knew that there is a powerful Law of Attraction between Boys and Dirt, and that you cannot interfere with the Laws of Nature.

She closed her eyes at the sight. Then she mastered her feelings and enquired faintly, "Where's Hubert, dears?"

William, his freckled face as expressionless as a mummy's, spoke in a mincingly polite tone of voice.

"Hubert said he was coming down in a minute and would we begin supper without him, please."

Aunt Emmy was taken aback.

She went to the bottom of the staircase. "Hubert, darling!" she called.

The real guests were still crouching behind packing cases in the attic waiting to be "found".

And Hubert's "Hey!" was too faint to reach Aunt Emmy's short hearing. The sight of the "guests" surging into the dining-room, recalled her to the scene of action.

"I think Hubert has gone to tidy himself," she said, "and I think, perhaps, you little boys should do the same."

The little boys ignored this suggestion, and, sitting down at the table, began to eat.

Aunt Emmy had always had a vague suspicion that she disliked boys, and the suspicion now grew to a certainty.

These boys refused bread and butter. They devoured iced cakes as fast as poor Aunt Emmy could hand them round. They

demanded trifle and blancmange and jelly.

They ate ravenously, as though it were some mighty task they had set themselves.

They got through enormous quantities of food.

They ate in silence, ignoring all Aunt Emmy's polite questions as to how they were getting on with their lessons at school.

They worked like Trojans. The dish of iced cakes was empty. The trifle dish was empty. The blancmange dish was empty. The cream cake dish was empty.

Only plates of plain bread and butter stood untouched.

Aunt Emmy looked at them aghast.

Louder and more indignant grew the Hubertian "Hey's!" from upstairs.

And another sound had joined them – a sound as of a pattering of many hands on a distant door.

The real guests had evidently awakened to the fact that something had gone wrong somewhere.

"Do you hear a – a – sort of *sound*?" said Aunt Emmy doubtfully, putting her hand to her ear. William looked up.

"What sort of a sound?" he demanded, fixing Aunt Emmy with his stern unblinking gaze.

"I – I think I'll go and see whatever dear Hubert's doing," said Aunt Emmy faintly, and she fled from the horrible spectacle of these ungentlemanly little boys.

William immediately opened the dining-room window, and the Outlaws, their bodies sated with the joy of the Laneite feast, their souls sated with the joy of vengeance, crept out into the night.

The Laneites had openly mocked them and spoilt their conjuring show. They had eaten the Laneites' supper.

An eye for an eye, a tooth for a tooth – a supper for a dead cat. They were quits.

Aunt Emmy found and rescued the in-furiated Laneites, brought them down to the Spartan remains left them by the Outlaws,

and then went away to have a nervous break-down quietly by herself.

Never would she have anything to do with boys again – never, never, *never*!

Mr Lane was not in the best of tempers when he returned home.

The vindictive cheerfulness and persistent healthiness of his aged relative had had a very embittering effect on him.

And the story of the Outlaws' marauding expedition proved to be the last straw.

So he sat down at once, and wrote a

very strong letter to the Outlaws' fathers.

The fathers of the Outlaws were quite accustomed to receiving strong letters from Mr Lane. And quite often the fathers did nothing at all beyond dropping the strong letter into the wastepaper basket.

But consuming vast quantities of Lane food uninvited was a serious matter, and the heavy hand of parental retribution descended upon the Outlaws that night.

But the effect of the heavy hand is always short-lived.

The next day the Outlaws sallied out undaunted. The Laneites glowered ferociously at the Outlaws in the village street.

"Ha, ha! *You* jolly well caught it last night," said Hubert derisively.

"Hush, darling!" said William, in a shrill falsetto. "Say it quietly. Little gentlemen never raise their voices."

"I'll tell my father," said Hubert, in fury.

"Don't take any notice of them," counselled Bertie Franks. "My mother told me never to have anything to do with them."

But the Outlaws now began to rub their hands round their stomachs, smacking their lips and screwing up their faces.

"Cream cakes," said William. "Coo, *jolly* good!"

"Trifle!" murmured Ginger, rapturously.

"Jelly and blancmange," said Douglas and Henry.

This was more than even the Hubert Laneites could stand.

Unwarlike as they were, accustomed to take their stand behind Mr Lane's strong letters, they threw caution to the winds, and hurled themselves to mortal combat with the Outlaws.

It was a good fight, and revealed un-suspected resources of courage and prowess in the Hubert Laneites.

It ended in a general mix-up of Outlaws and Laneites in a muddy ditch.

There Outlaws and Laneites sat up panting

and covered with mud, and looked at each other.

And slowly over the faces of all dawned a grin of satisfaction.

"Go home and tell your father now," said William to Hubert.

And Hubert, swelling with pride and joy after his first real fight, said, "No, I won't. An' – an' we'll fight you again," and added hastily (for though he'd enjoyed it he'd had quite enough for one day), "tomorrow."

Meet Just William

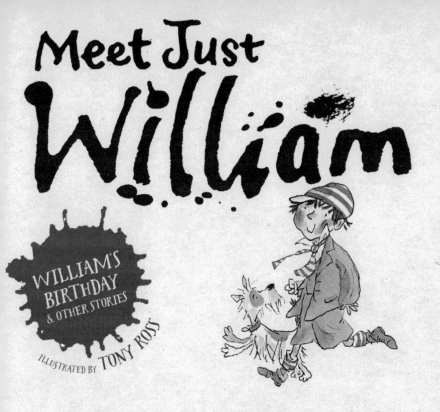

WILLIAM'S BIRTHDAY & OTHER STORIES

ILLUSTRATED BY TONY ROSS

William Brown is always getting up to mischief!
Whether it's hunting for hidden treasure in Miss
Peache's garden or putting a snowman on trial, there's
never a dull moment with William Brown around.

RICHMAL CROMPTON
ADAPTED BY MARTIN JARVIS

Two Meet Just William books in one featuring the
funniest stories about William Brown, specially
adapted for younger readers by Martin Jarvis —
the 'voice of William' on radio!

Coming soon

Meet Just William

WILLIAM'S HAUNTED HOUSE & OTHER STORIES

ILLUSTRATED BY TONY ROSS

William returns! Whether he's having a midnight
feast with the Outlaws or causing trouble
with Ginger, there's never a dull moment with
William Brown around.

RICHMAL CROMPTON
ADAPTED BY MARTIN JARVIS

Two Meet Just William books in one featuring the
funniest stories about William Brown, specially
adapted for younger readers by Martin Jarvis –
the 'voice of William' on radio!